moon

For Frank, who loves adventures too.

First Edition 2011
Kane Miller, A Division of EDC Publishing

Text and illustrations copyright © Lindsay Ward, 2010

All rights reserved.

For information contact:
Kane Miller, A Division of EDC Publishing
PO Box 470663
Tulsa, OK 74147-0663
www.kanemiller.com
www.edcpub.com

Library of Congress Control Number: 2010921031

Printed and bound in Malaysia by Tien Wah Press Pte. Ltd.
1 2 3 4 5 6 7 8 9 10

ISBN: 978-1-935279-77-8

earth
earth
earth
earth
earth
earth
earth
earth

Pelly and Mr. Harrison Visit the Moon

Lindsay Ward

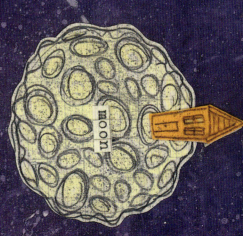

moon

Kane Miller
A DIVISION OF EDC PUBLISHING

One evening, just before bedtime, as Pelly was brushing her teeth with Mr. Harrison, she noticed something peculiar.

There was a rocket engine attached to the end of the bathtub.

Well, that's odd. I don't remember ever seeing this here before.

Mr. Harrison jumped into the tub, wagging his tail excitedly.

All right, Mr. Harrison, where should we go?

Mr. Harrison looked out the window and barked at the moon.

As soon as Pelly stepped into the tub, two helmets appeared, and a steering wheel grew up from the drain.

The engine roared to life as the bathtub shrunk down just small enough to fly through the window.

Pelly and Mr. Harrison flew higher and higher and higher over the city, through the clouds, and up into outer space.

The tub gently floated down to the moon.

Pelly and Mr. Harrison were exploring when they noticed a little alien watching them.

The alien waved and grabbed Pelly's hand, leading her and

Mr. Harrison into a huge crater with a row of houses in the center.

salt

sugar

flour

moon
dust

moon pie

Pelly and Mr. Harrison followed the little alien inside.

There in the kitchen, making the most delicious smelling moon pies, was another alien.

After they filled up on moon pies, the little alien took Pelly and Mr. Harrison back outside where she showed them all the best things about living on the moon...

GRAVITY LEAPING.

moon

moon

moon

moon

moon

moon

They learned about gravity leaping, which Mr. Harrison excelled in rather quickly.

Spaceship racing.

Moon rock digging.

Star catching.

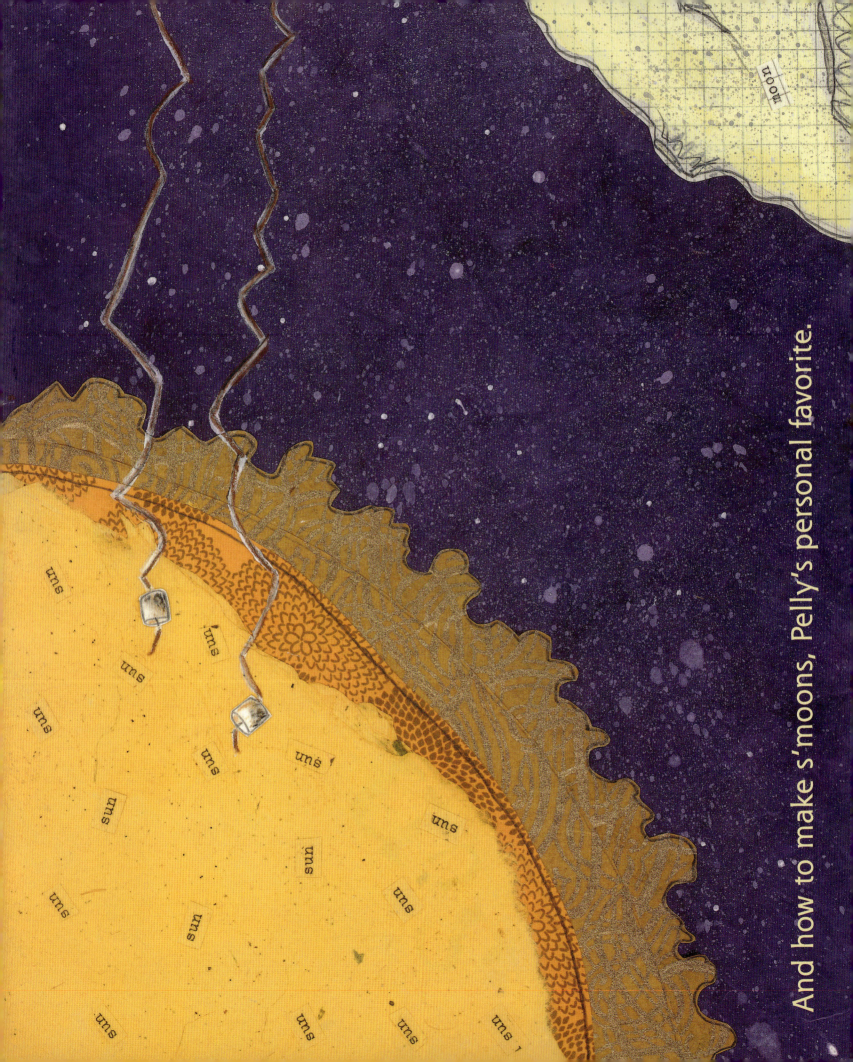

And how to make s'moons, Pelly's personal favorite.

moon

sun

Pelly noticed it was getting late.

The little alien walked Pelly and Mr. Harrison
back to their bathtub.

It was time to say goodbye.

Pelly and Mr. Harrison got into the bathtub and floated back down to earth. The little alien grew smaller and smaller in the distance.

That night, Pelly and Mr. Harrison dreamed of warm s'moons.

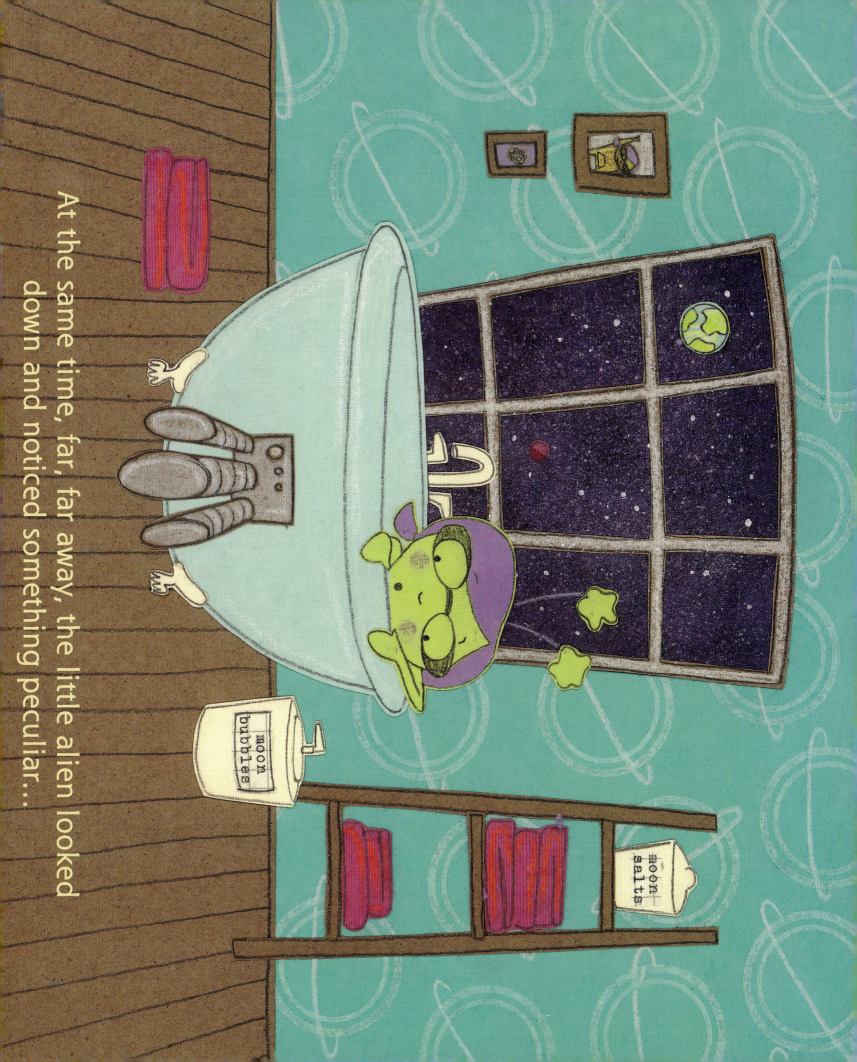

At the same time, far, far, far away, the little alien looked down and noticed something peculiar...